For information regarding permission, write to
Jessica Aguilera at: loveandpaper7@gmail.com
Text and art copyright © 2014 by Jessica Aguilera.
All rights reserved.

Published in collaboration with
Fortitude Graphic Design & Printing and Season Press LLC.

ISBN: 10-0-9741611-2-8
ISBN: 13-978-0-9741611-2-9

Aguilera, Jessica, 1972- Rose/ by Jessica Aguilera

Summary: Rose's unique style expresses the importance of individuality.

Jessica Aguilera uses paper art to create this story.

Printed in the United States of America

First Edition

10 9 8 7 6 5 4 3 2 1

Dedication
To my Mom, from whom I get my love of reading.
To my Dad, from whom I get my love of stargazing.
Thank you for everything. I love you.
J.A.

This is Rose.

Rose is excited! She has just received an invitation to a birthday party for her friend, Libby.

She went to her local bookstore and picked out a present for Libby - a big picture book all about trees.

When she got home, she made
a birthday card for Libby.
She drew a picture of an
apple tree on the front.

Now all there was left
to do was to find the
perfect outfit!

Rose thought carefully.

"Should I wear the yellow dress from my Auntie's wedding?

The orange polkadot dress that I wore on the first day of school? Or should I wear...?"

My green dress
with the
   pink heart?

My purple dress
with the
yellow zigzags?

Or, my light blue
sweater with the
dark blue buttons?

Rose liked all of these, but she wanted to wear something extra special to the party.

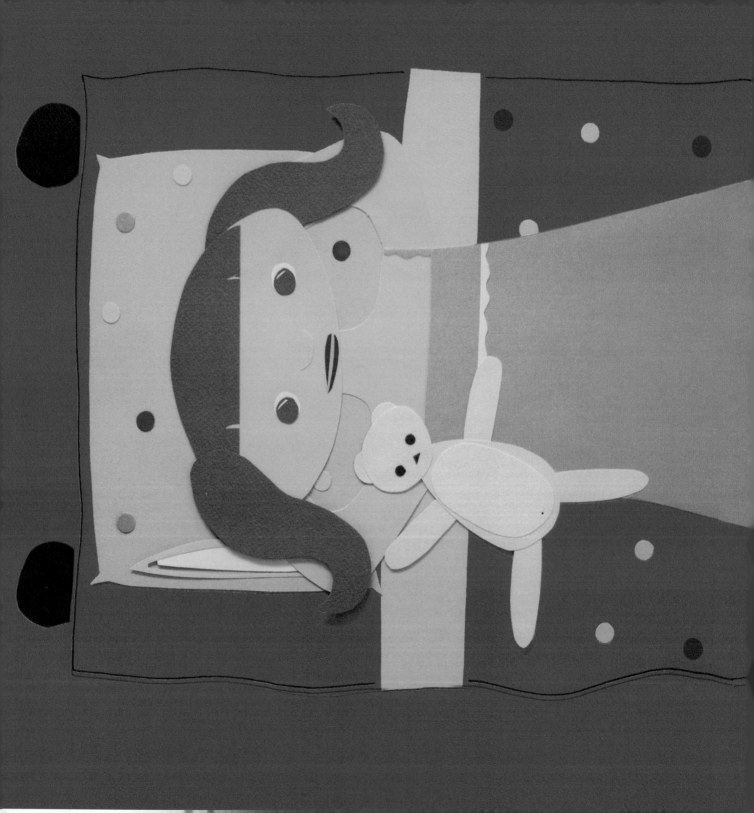

As Rose drifted
off to sleep,
her eyes popped
open.

"I know what
I'll wear!"

Rose woke up early the next morning and quickly slipped into her special outfit.

She couldn't wait to show her mom!

"So Mom,
what do you think?"
Her mom looked at her
in surprise.
"You're wearing
your brother's suit
to the party?" her
mom asked.

"Yes!
Don't you like it?"

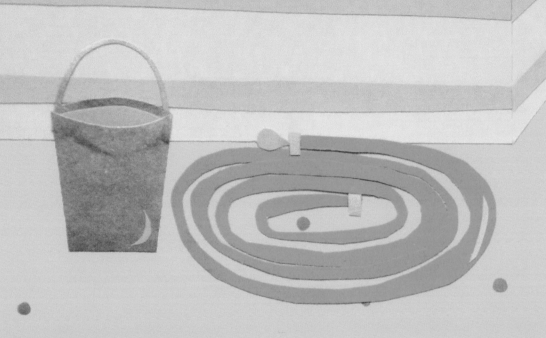

"It's definitely interesting," her mom said.
"But I'm not sure. Something seems to be
missing. Maybe you should try…"

"A pretty bow tie?"

"A pair of sparkly earrings?"

"Or a shiny pearl necklace?"

Her mom shook her head.
"No. These
things aren't right,"
she said.

She sighed and thought
for a moment...

She fiddled with this...

She fiddled with that...

"Perfect! A rose for a Rose," her mom said, laughing.
Rose looked down to see that her mom had pinned a perfect pink
rose to her suit. "So, what do YOU think?" her mom asked.
"I think I'm ready for a party!" said Rose.

Libby's gift...

As Rose left for the party, she made sure she had...

Libby's birthday card...

Her matching purse...

And her rose, of course!

Rose saw all of her friends at the party.

"This is fun!"

"Yummy cake!"

"Happy Birthday, Libby!"

"Best birthday ever!"

Everyone had a very 'rosy' time.

Writing, illustrating and publishing a children's book has been a longtime dream for author Jessica Aguilera. This book was written to inspire children to embrace their individuality and to always stay true to themselves. It is also a demonstration of how art can be created using the simplest of supplies...paper, scissors, and glue.

Jessica lives in Kalamazoo, Michigan where she enjoys long walks with her dog Milo, dancing with friends, eating cake with her family, and treasure hunts in the woods. This is her first book.

For more information contact Jessica Aguilera at: loveandpaper7@gmail.com.